T#: 471905

randomhousekids.com

ISBN 978-0-399-55350-9

MANUFACTURED IN CHINA

10 9 8 7 6 5 4 3 2 1

a Little Golden Book® Collection

Nine

nickelodeon™

Tales

A GOLDEN BOOK • NEW YORK

Contents

ITTY-
BITTY
KITTY
RESCUE

It was a warm, sunny day. Chase and Rubble were having a great time playing catch at the beach. Then they heard a far-off cry.

"*Meow! Meow!*"

A kitten was clinging to a toy boat out in the water!

"Uh-oh!" Rubble exclaimed. "That little kitty is in trouble."

"We need to tell Ryder," Chase said.

Chase and Rubble raced to the Lookout to tell
Ryder about the kitty.
"No job is too big, no pup is too small!"
declared Ryder. He pushed a button on his
PupPad and sounded the PAW Patrol Alarm.

Minutes later, Marshall, Skye, Rocky, and Zuma
joined their puppy pals at the Lookout.

"PAW Patrol is ready for action," reported
Chase, sitting at attention.

"A kitten is floating out to sea," Ryder announced, pointing to the viewing screen behind him.

"We have to save the itty-bitty kitty!" exclaimed Rubble. Then he straightened up and added, "I mean, ahem, we have to save the kitten."

"Zuma, your hovercraft is perfect for a water rescue," Ryder said.

"Ready, set, get wet!" Zuma barked.

"And, Skye," Ryder continued, "I'll need you and your helicopter to help find the kitten quickly."

"This pup's got to fly!" Skye exclaimed.

Zuma's hovercraft splashed across Adventure Bay. Ryder turned his ATV into a Jet Ski and followed. Up above, Sky zoomed through the air. She quickly spotted the kitten.

"We're here to help you," Ryder said, easing his Jet Ski to a stop.

The little kitten jumped from her boat and landed on Zuma's head. The startled pup fell into the water.

Zuma yelled, "Don't touch the—"

The kitten accidentally hit the throttle and raced off on the hovercraft.

The hovercraft zoomed around the bay.
Overhead, Skye turned this way and that, trying
to follow the hovercraft's twisting course.

"This kitty is making me dizzy," she groaned.

Ryder pulled up next to the hovercraft and
jumped on board. He stopped the engine and
gently picked up the shivering kitten.

"Everything's all right," he said, pulling a slimy
piece of seaweed off the kitten. "Let's take you
back to dry land and get you cleaned up."

Later that day, Rubble skateboarded into Katie's Pet Parlor with his new BFF. "Aww, whose cute kitty is that?" Katie asked. "We don't know," Rubble explained. "We found her on the bay with no collar or tags, just this purple ribbon."

"Does the kitty-widdy
want a nice warm bath?"
Rubble asked.

"*Meow*," the kitten replied.

"Do you want me to do it?" Katie asked.
"Cats can be a little tricky to bathe."

"Tricky?" Rubble said. "Not this little sweetie."

But the kitten had other ideas. The moment she touched the water, she jumped away with a screech.

She scurried along shelves, knocking over bottles of shampoo.

Rubble slipped on a spinning bottle.

The kitten fell onto Rubble's skateboard
and rolled out the door!

15

Down the street from Katie's Pet Parlor, Ryder got a message from Rocky: *"A little girl is looking for her lost kitty named Precious."*

Ryder recognized the kitten in the picture the girl was holding. Before he could say a word, Precious rolled past on Rubble's skateboard. She skated down a hill and disappeared into town.

"Chase, it's time to use your Super Sniffer!"
Ryder said.

Chase needed something with the kitty's scent
on it. Luckily, they had her purple ribbon.

Chase took a deep sniff. "She went that way—
ACHOO! Sorry. Cat hair makes me sneeze."

Sniff, sniff, sniff.

Chase followed the scent until he found
Rubble's skateboard at the bottom of the town
hall steps.

"Good sniffing," Ryder said.

Ryder and the pups looked around and saw
a shocking sight.

The kitty was inside the town hall bell tower!

Ryder pulled out his PupPad and called for
Marshall and his fire truck.

"I'm all fired up!" Marshall said as his fire truck screeched to a halt in front of the town hall. He arrived at the same time as the kitty's owner.

Ryder told Marshall to put up his ladder. "We need to get the kitten down from that tower."

"I'm on it," Marshall declared. He extended the truck's ladder and carefully started to climb.

Marshall reached the top of the ladder.
The scared little kitten was clinging
desperately to a rope in the tower.

"I'll get you down safely," Marshall said.
"Come here."

"*Meow,*" Precious whimpered.

The kitten jumped from the rope. She tried to grab Marshall's helmet but missed—and clutched his face instead.

"Whoa!" Marshall yelped. He couldn't see!

The ladder shook. Marshall lost his grip. He and the kitten fell off the ladder!

Ryder caught Marshall, and the little kitty tumbled into her owner's arms.

"Precious!" the girl exclaimed. "You're okay! You owe these brave pups a thank-you for all their help."

"Whenever you need us," Ryder said, "just yelp for help!"

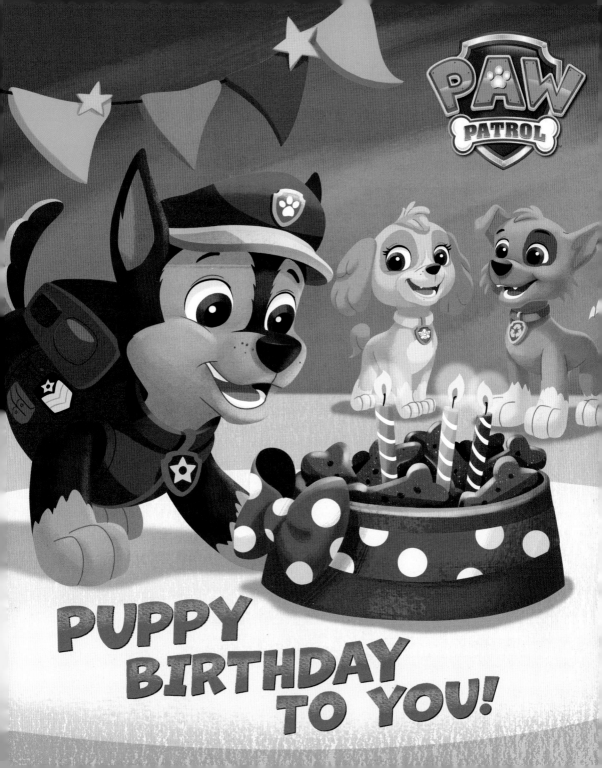

One windy afternoon in Adventure Bay, a box moved down the street toward Katie's Pet Parlor. But this box wasn't being blown by the wind. *It was creeping down the street on eight paws!*

Suddenly, a big gust blew the box away, revealing Skye and Rubble underneath. They quickly scampered into the shop.

Inside, Ryder, Katie, and Rocky were getting ready for Chase's surprise birthday party.

"Who's making sure Chase doesn't surprise *us* while we set up?" Skye asked.

"Marshall," Rocky said. "He can keep a secret— can't he?"

Across town, Marshall and Chase were playing in Pup Park. They swung on the swings and slid down the slide.

"Maybe we should go find Ryder and the pups," Chase said.

"No!" Marshall protested. "We can't! Because it's, um, so nice out."

Just then, the wind picked up again and blew them right across the park!

Back at the Pet Parlor, the lights suddenly went dark, and Katie's mixer stopped.

"All the lights on the street are out!" Rocky yelped.

Ryder thought he knew what was wrong. "PAW Patrol, to the Lookout!"

The team raced to the Lookout. But without electricity, the doors wouldn't open. Luckily, Rocky had a screwdriver, which did the trick.

Once they were inside, Ryder used his
telescope to check Adventure Bay's windmills.
   "Just as I thought," he said. "The wind broke
a propeller. Since the windmill can't turn, it can't
make electricity. We need to fix it!"

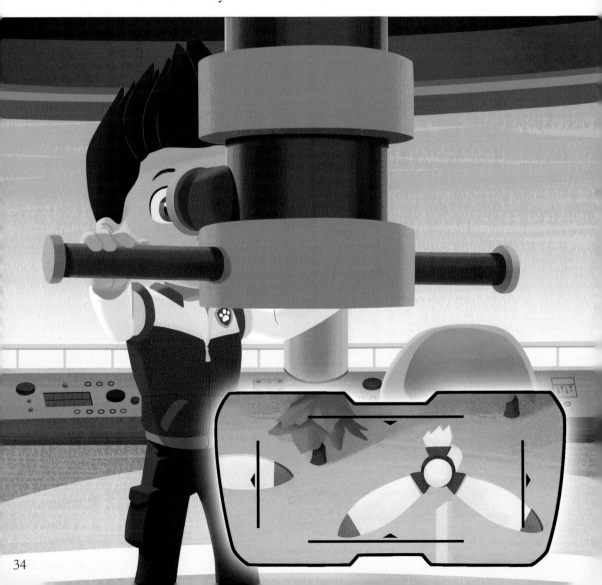

Ryder looked at Rocky. "We'll need something
from your truck to fix the broken blade."

"Green means go!" Rocky said, preparing
for action.

"We'll need Marshall's ladder to climb up and fix the windmill," said Ryder.

Marshall nodded. "I'm fired up!"

"Chase, the traffic lights won't work without electricity," Ryder continued. "I need you to use your siren and megaphone to direct traffic."

"These paws uphold the laws," Chase declared.

Meanwhile, Skye, Zuma, and Rubble raced
back to the Pet Parlor to continue setting up for
Chase's surprise party. It was very dark, but Katie
had a flashlight.

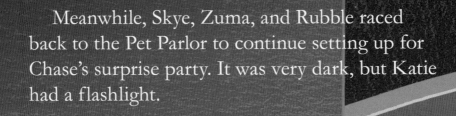

At the center of town, Chase busily directed traffic.
"You're our hero," Mayor Goodway said as she
crossed the street safely.
"I'm just doing my PAW Patrol duty," Chase said.

Up in the hills, Ryder, Marshall, and Rocky
went to work on the broken windmill. Ryder
climbed Marshall's ladder and removed the old
blade while Rocky looked for a replacement piece.
   "No, not a tire . . . not a lawn chair," Rocky
said, pulling stuff out of his truck. At last he found
what he wanted. "Here it is—my old surfboard!"

"This surfboard will catch a breeze and help turn it into electricity," Rocky said as he bolted the board into place. The wind picked up and the windmill started to turn. Lights came on all over Adventure Bay!

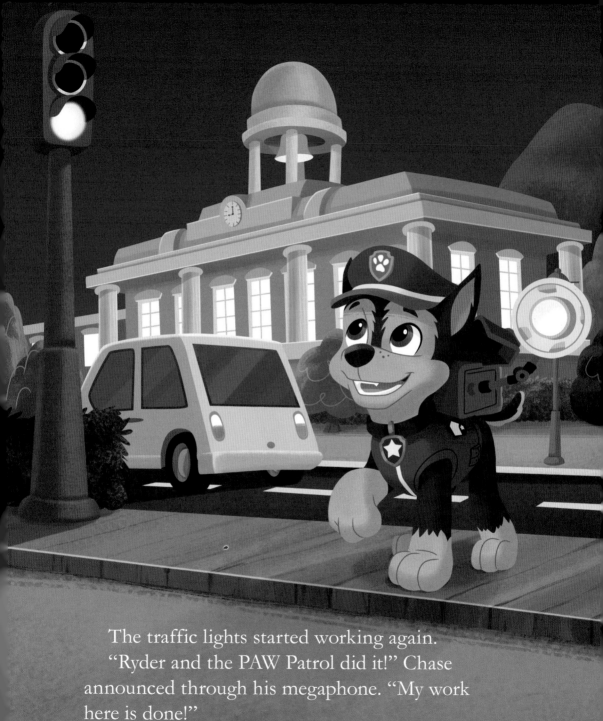

The traffic lights started working again. "Ryder and the PAW Patrol did it!" Chase announced through his megaphone. "My work here is done!"

The lights in the Pet Parlor glowed brightly.
"Hooray!" cheered Skye, but then she
frowned. "Aw! There's no time to make a cake."
Katie thought for a moment. "I have an idea!"

As Chase drove back to the
Lookout, he got a call from Ryder.
"We need you at Katie's—
in a hurry!"

When Chase got
there, everything
was dark and quiet.

Chase stepped inside. The lights went on. "SURPRISE!" everyone yelled.

Chase was amazed. "Wow! You guys turned the lights back on AND made a party for me?"

"We didn't have time to bake you a real cake," Katie said, "so we hope you like your pup-treat cookie cake."

"Whenever it's your birthday, just yelp for help!" Ryder said with a laugh.
All the puppies cheered and enjoyed a taste of Chase's special cake.

IT'S TIME FOR BUBBLE PUPPY!

One morning, Gil was on his way to school when he heard barking.

"I hear puppies!" he said.

Gil followed the barks and found a whole *bunch* of puppies!

"These puppies are up for adoption," explained a friendly lady snail. "That means we're looking for people to take them home and give them nice places to live."

"I wish I had a puppy like that one," Gil said, pointing to a cute little guy with orange spots that was barking happily. The puppy was friendly—and really good at chasing bubbles!

When Gil got to school, he told his friends Molly, Goby, Oona, Deema, and Nonny all about the puppy. "I wish I could adopt him," he said.

"Adopting a pet is a great thing to do," said their teacher, Mr. Grouper. "You just have to find the right pet for you."

"I want a cat that says *meow*," said Molly.

"I want a parrot!" said Deema.

"I like guinea pigs!" said Goby.

"I think that puppy would be perfect for me," Gil said. "We'd be best buddies. He'd lick my face to wake me up every morning, and we would run and play in the park all the time!"

"But Gil, you can't play with
the puppy all the time," Molly said.
"You have to take care of him, too."

"That's right," Mr. Grouper said.
"Taking care of a pet is a really big job."

"If your puppy is hungry, you'll have to give it food to eat," Mr. Grouper said.

"And puppies get thirsty, too, so they
need lots of water," said Molly.

"And when your puppy needs to go outside," said Goby, "you'll put him on a leash and take him for a walk!"

"If that puppy was my pet, I would take really good care of him," said Gil.

"You would?" said Mr. Grouper. "Well, then come with me. Everybody, let's line up. I have something to show you!"

Mr. Grouper led the class through their
watery world. Finally, they arrived at the
puppy adoption center!

"This is where I met that puppy!" said Gil.

But when Gil looked for the
puppies, they were all gone!

The lady snail told him that
all the puppies had been
adopted—including Gil's favorite!
Gil was very sad.

"Here, you'll need these," said the lady snail,
handing Gil a bowl and a leash.
"But why?" asked Gil.

"Because he's coming back to class with us!" said Mr. Grouper. "We adopted him!"

"*Arf! Arf!*" barked the happy little puppy.

All the Bubble Guppies cheered. "Yay! Thank you, Mr. Grouper!"

Everyone was very excited about their new pet.

They all agreed to help take care of the new puppy.

"I'll give him baths," said Gil.

"And I'll take him out for walks," said Goby.

Molly and Nonny couldn't wait to feed the puppy and give him water.

Oona said she would train the puppy.

"And I'll hug him!" promised Deema.

"But what should we call him?" asked Molly.

"Arf!" barked the puppy, and a big bubble came out of his mouth!

"I know," said Gil. "Let's call him . . . BUBBLE PUPPY!"

Everyone thought Bubble Puppy was a wonderful name. They all took turns hugging Bubble Puppy, and he licked them all back.

Gil gave Bubble Puppy a really big hug. "I'm glad we adopted you, boy," he said.

"*Arf!*" barked Bubble Puppy. He was happy to have a nice new home with all his new friends, the Bubble Guppies.

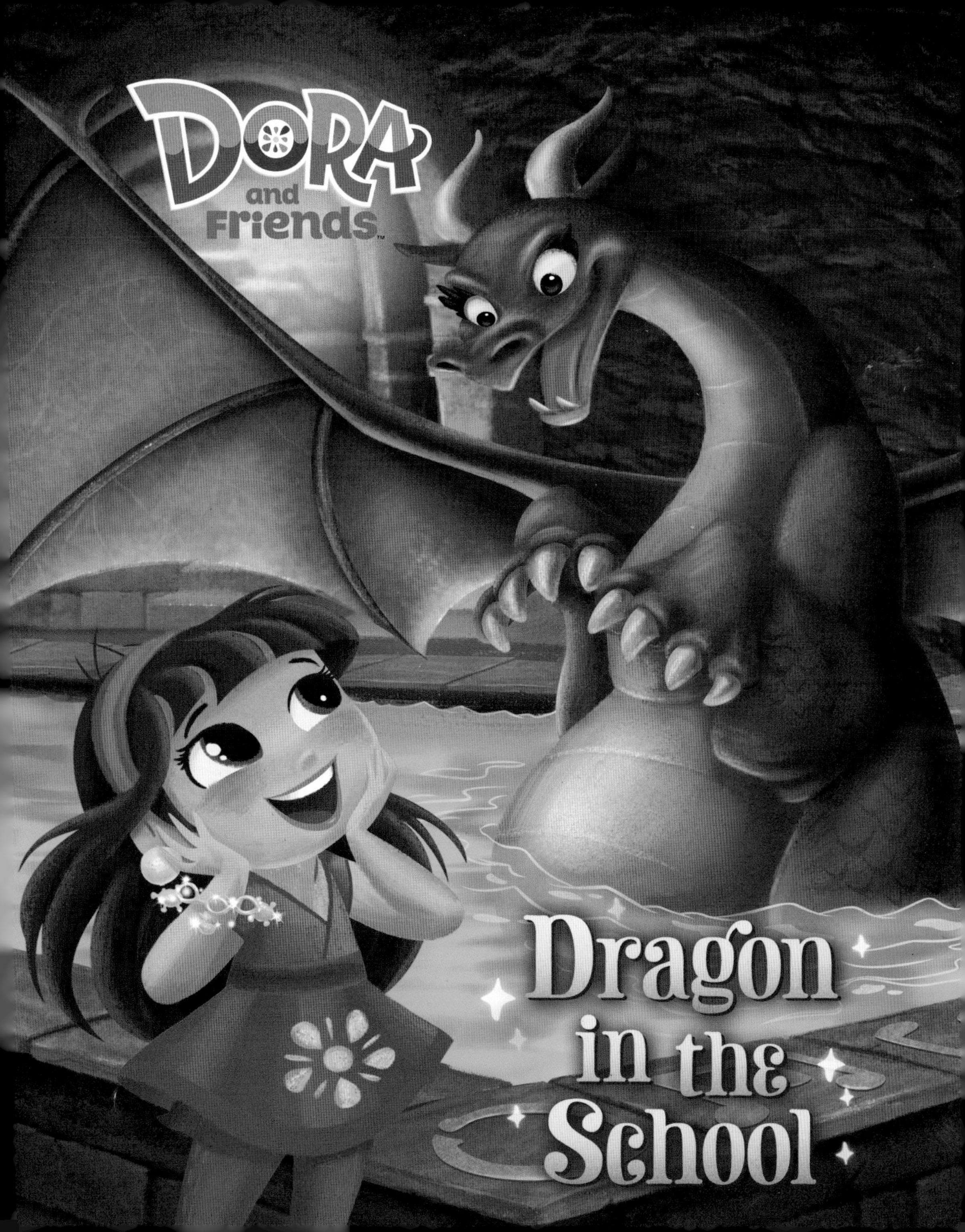

DORA and **Friends**

Dragon in the School

One afternoon outside their school,
Dora and Naiya noticed Pablo heading inside.
   "You're not searching for that ancient pool
again, are you?" Dora asked.
   "I have to find out if the stories are true,"
Pablo said.

Naiya and Dora joined Pablo. They came upon a secret passageway that led to a dead end.

"*¡Sigue buscando!*" said Dora. "Keep looking! You never know what you might find."

The friends discovered a secret door. "*¡Ábrete, puerta!*" they called—and the door opened!

The friends went down a set of stairs . . .
and found the ancient pool!

As Pablo jumped in, Dora and Naiya studied
a mural on the wall. It told the story of a girl
and a dragon. . . .

The girl and the dragon lived on a beautiful island. Other dragons came to make the island their home, too!

One day, a wizard appeared. He wanted the dragons for himself, so he cast a spell and took all the dragons away.

The girl left the island and went to Dora's school in Playa Verde.

Shortly after, the wizard arrived with his dragons. He wanted to take over the school!

But the big dragon recognized the girl and chased the wizard away!

"I wonder whatever happened to that big dragon," said Pablo. Just then, bubbles appeared around him. Something was coming up from the bottom!

It was the big dragon!

"Let's get out of here!" cried Pablo.

But Dora ran over to the dragon. She put her hands on her heart. "The dragon needs to know we're friends. *¡Somos amigos!*"

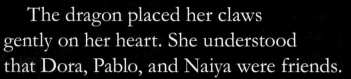

The dragon placed her claws
gently on her heart. She understood
that Dora, Pablo, and Naiya were friends.
"I think she's protecting something," said
Dora. Suddenly, tiny bubbles appeared on the
water as a baby dragon rose from the pool.

While the baby dragon joined his
mama, they all heard a huge crash.
The mean wizard had returned!
"I want my dragon back!" he cried.

"Go to your home!" Dora told Mama Dragon, pointing to the island on the mural.

Mama Dragon gave her baby to Dora to protect. Then she flew up through the ceiling. When the wizard took off after her, Dora and her friends escaped with the baby dragon.

All of Dora's friends wanted to help
return the baby dragon to his mama.
They found a map that led to the
dragon's island home. They boarded a
ship, hoisted the sails, and set off.

As they sailed through the water,
Emma and Pablo spotted the wizard.
He was heading to the island, too!

The friends sped to the island and landed
on a sandy beach. Then they saw the wizard
flying toward them!

"We've got to find somewhere to hide!"
exclaimed Dora.

The friends found a cave and ran inside.

In the darkness, the baby dragon
began to call for his mama.

"*Eee-ee-eeee!*" he squeaked. His cries
loosened the cave walls!

"Rockslide!" yelled Pablo.

The friends were trapped!

Everyone started to dig—except Pablo.
"Guys, I think Mama Dragon is here in
the cave with us," he whispered.

"Something's glowing up ahead!"
called Pablo.

Dora shined a light—right onto Mama
Dragon! She was having trouble getting
up. Her wing was hurt!

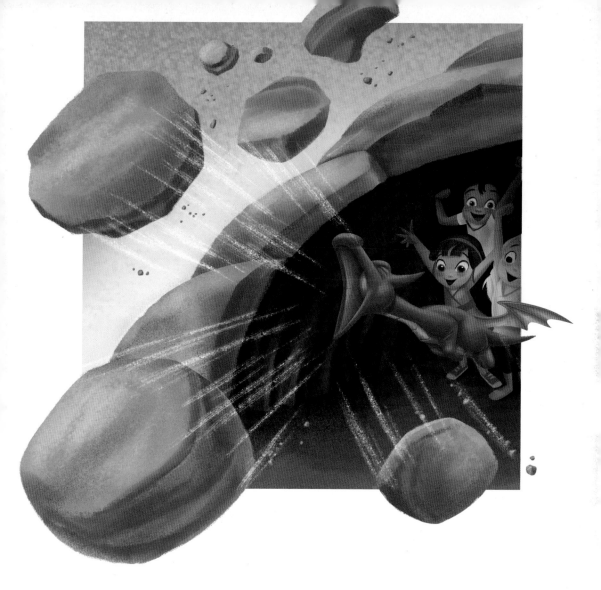

Naiya examined the wing. "I'll need an aloe plant and volcano mud to heal her."

The baby dragon wanted to help. He rushed to the blocked cave entrance and roared so loudly that he cleared away the rocks!

Working together, the friends collected the aloe plant and volcano mud. Alana took them inside and gave them to Naiya. The others were about to follow when the wizard flew down.

"A little dragon! I've always wanted one!" The wizard raised his hands to cast a spell.

Mama Dragon burst from the cave with a roar. Naiya had fixed her wing!

The wizard summoned his other dragons to face Mama Dragon.

"We need help," said Dora. She held out her magic charm bracelet, which had a unicorn charm on it. *"¡Unicornio mágico!"*

When the wizard's dragons
saw the unicorn, they stopped
their attack. Long ago, dragons
and unicorns had made a truce.

Then the dragons roared and broke the wizard's wand so he couldn't cast a spell again. The defeated wizard hung his head. "I've always wanted to be friends with the dragons," he said softly.

Dora nodded. "You have to ask them."

The wizard put his hands to his heart. *"¿Somos amigos?"* he asked.

Mama Dragon nodded happily.

"We saved the dragons!" cried the friends. *"¡Todos juntos!"*

SHIMMER and Shine™

Backyard Ballet

Leah and Zac were twirling and leaping around Leah's living room. They had just seen *Swan Lake,* and they were practicing to put on their own ballet!

Leah spun and lost her balance. Zac crashed into the couch!

"I guess we need more practice," Leah giggled.

Zac grinned. "How about you practice spinning and I practice leaping? Later we can dance *Swan Lake* together!"

After Zac left to practice on his own, Leah sighed.
"If only I could dance like the real Swan Queen."
Suddenly, she had an idea!

Leah summoned Shimmer and Shine, twin genies-in-training who could grant her three wishes a day.

"I wish I was the Swan Queen!" Leah declared.

"*Boom, Zahramay!* First wish of the day!" chanted Shine.

Leah found herself dressed as the Swan Queen from the ballet—but with six loud swans as royal subjects!

"I was hoping to spin like the *ballerina* Swan Queen, not be the actual queen of six swans!" she said.

Shine frowned. "Oh, sounds like I made a mistake."

Leah smiled. "It's okay, Shine. Sometimes mistakes happen. Maybe these swans won't get in the way of spinning practice!"

But having six swans in Leah's living room
turned into a giant honking disaster!

Leah had to get the swans outside before they destroyed the whole house.

"I wish the swans would follow me!" she cried. Shimmer jangled her magic bracelets. *"Boom, Zahramay! Second wish of the day!"*

Now the swans followed Leah's every move,
whether she turned her head or hopped on one foot.
Though it wasn't what she had wished for, she loved it!
The swans lined up and followed her to the backyard.

Leah had saved her home from the swans, but she had forgotten to practice for the ballet performance!

She closed her eyes and made her final wish.
"I wish to be a ballerina in *Swan Lake*!"

When Leah opened her eyes, she was standing on a rock, surrounded by lily pads. Her backyard had been transformed into a giant lake!

She looked around. "This is beautiful, but I wanted to dance like the ballerina from *Swan Lake,* not have an actual lake."

Shine hung her head. "Sorry, Leah. I didn't mean to make such a big mistake."

Leah hugged Shine. "It's okay. No mistake is too big to fix. Even one as big as a lake!"

Leah started to inch off the rock. "Let's get back to dry land so we can practice spinning!" Suddenly, she slipped!

As Leah fell, she bounced off a lily pad and did
a perfect ballerina spin!

"I don't know if you meant to do that, but it was
amazing!" said Shine.

Leah kept bouncing and spinning from pad to pad. The swans did the same.

"If I practice more," she said, "maybe I'll finally spin like the Swan Queen!"

For the rest of the afternoon, Leah, the genies,
and the swans practiced ballet on the lily pads.

Late in the day, Zac poked his head through a loose board in the fence. Shimmer and Shine quickly hid, but he didn't even notice them.

"Whoa!" he shouted to Leah. "There's a lake in your backyard!"

Zac had been practicing his leaps and was
ready for the show. "You've got everything we need—
the swans, the Swan Lake, and the Swan Queen!"

"I'm still missing one more piece." Leah held out her hand. "The best leaper ever! Wanna dance?"
Together the two friends put on a magical performance!

After the show, Leah found Shimmer and Shine.
"We fixed our mistakes, and the day turned out great!"
She hugged the two genies. "See you tomorrow?"

"Abso-*genie*-lutely!" chimed Shimmer and Shine.

room! Blaze raced across the countryside.

"Let's head for that hill, Blaze! I bet it would make an awesome jump," said AJ. He was Blaze's best friend—and the best driver a Monster Machine could have.

"Give me some speed!" Blaze cheered. AJ pressed the pedal. They raced up the hill and shot into the air!

123

Blaze and AJ landed in Axle City.

"Hubcaps! I've never seen so many Monster Machines!" Blaze said. "They're all driving to the Monsterdome to see the big championship race!"

"Let's go get a closer look," said AJ.

Inside the Monsterdome, Blaze and AJ
met Gabby.

"I'm a mechanic," she said. "I fix all the
Monster Machines. Would you like to meet
some of the racers?"

Blaze and AJ met Stripes the tiger truck. He had special claws on his tires that made him great at climbing.

They met Starla, a cowgirl truck who could do rope tricks.

126

They met Darington,
the amazing stunt truck . . .

and Zeg the dinosaur truck,
who loved to smash
and bash.

"Out of my way! Me first, me first!" said a big truck as he pushed past the others.

"His name is Crusher," Gabby said. "He thinks he's the best racer ever."

A small truck named Pickle pulled up next to Crusher. "I cannot wait to see who will win the big race," Pickle said. "It could be anyone!"

"No, Pickle—it's going to be me, me, me!" announced Crusher. Then he whispered to himself, "Because I'm going to cheat!"

A hatch on Crusher's side opened, and his Trouble Bubble Wand popped out. It blew big bubbles that captured Darington, Starla, Stripes, Zeg, and even Blaze. They began to float away.

The bubbles floated across the countryside. When Blaze's bubble finally popped, he landed in the Badlands, far from Axle City. Stripes landed nearby—but he was stuck in some vines, hanging from a cliff!

"Gaskets!" Blaze exclaimed. "We have to get to Stripes fast!"

Blaze saw that the rocks
were shaped like ramps.

He and AJ jumped
from one to the
other. The steeper
the ramp, the
higher they
went!

Finally, they reached the top and saved Stripes.

As the trucks rolled through a forest, Grizzly Trucks started to chase them. They had to escape, but the only way out was cut off by a river.

Blaze thought for a moment. "To get across, we need something we can float on."

The trucks found a rock and a piece of wood and pushed them into the water. The rock sank right away.

"But the wood is floating!" Blaze said. "We can get across on it!"

The trucks jumped onto the wood and floated to the other side of the river.

The trucks sped along a snowy mountainside. They saw Zeg just as his bubble popped. He fell to the ground and tumbled down a steep, icy hill.

"Let's *blaaaze*!" shouted AJ and Blaze. They raced down the hill and caught Zeg at the edge of the cliff with Blaze's tow hook.

"Zeg so happy!" Zeg cheered. "Blaze save Zeg!"

There was one last Monster Machine to find! The trucks drove through a cave and found Starla at the bottom of a hole.

"We'll get you out!" Blaze shouted down to her.

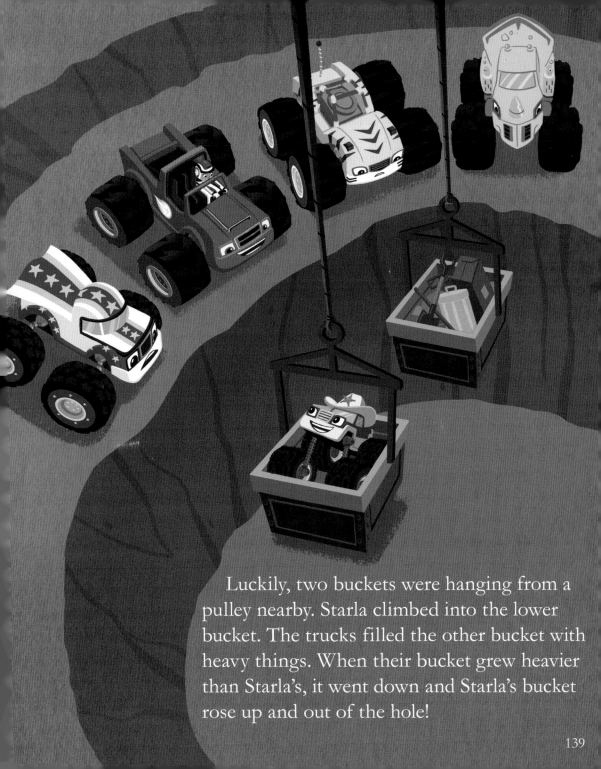

Luckily, two buckets were hanging from a pulley nearby. Starla climbed into the lower bucket. The trucks filled the other bucket with heavy things. When their bucket grew heavier than Starla's, it went down and Starla's bucket rose up and out of the hole!

The trucks zoomed back to the Monsterdome.
They arrived just as the race was about to start.
"Good luck out there," Blaze said.
"You should be in the race, too," Stripes said.

Blaze was amazed. "You really want me to race with you?"

"Blaze *friend*!" Zeg said.

"All right!" Blaze cheered. "AJ and I will do it together!"

"And they're off!" said Bump Bumperman, the announcer. The Monster Machines revved and roared and raced around the track.

But Crusher didn't want anyone else to win. One by one, he tried to knock the other racers out of his way, but there was one racer he couldn't get past.

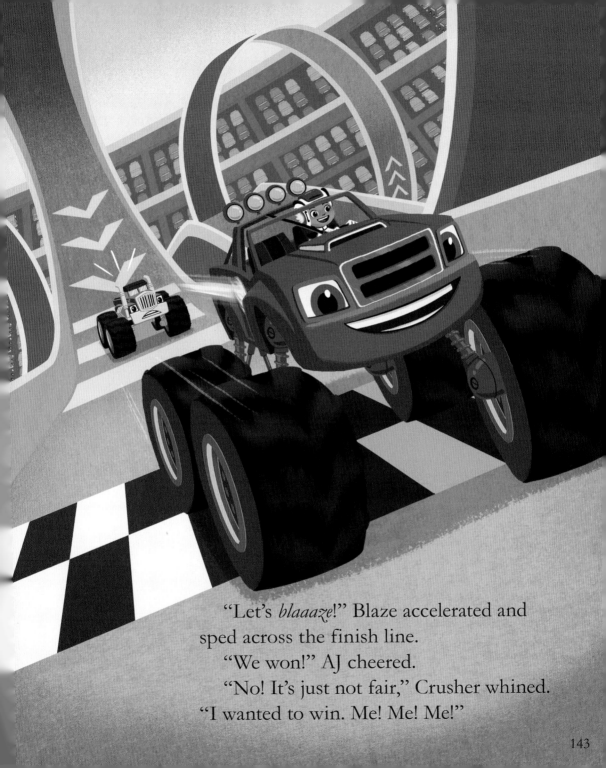

"Let's *blaaaze!*" Blaze accelerated and sped across the finish line.

"We won!" AJ cheered.

"No! It's just not fair," Crusher whined. "I wanted to win. Me! Me! Me!"

"Blaze! You're the Monster Machine World Champion,"
Bump Bumperman said. "What will you do next?"

"I'd like to hang out with my new friends," Blaze said.

The Monster Machines cheered as they took a victory
lap around the track with their new friend, Blaze.

One morning at the Axle City Garage,
Blaze and AJ were helping their friend
Gabby unload a shipment of tires.

"They're silly tires!" Gabby explained
with a giggle.

Inside the crates were dancing tires . . . stinky tires . . . and even feathery chicken tires!

"*Bok-bok-bok!*" clucked the tires as they rolled away.

Blaze and AJ saw Zeg trying to drive down the street. He was having a hard time because his tires had big holes in them!

Blaze pulled out his towing hook. "Hang on," he said. "I'll give you a tow!"

Suddenly, a crate wiggled and jiggled and then burst open! *Boing! Boing!* Four bright green silly tires bounced out.

"Funny tires go up and down," the dinosaur truck laughed. "Zeg like! Zeg want those tires!"

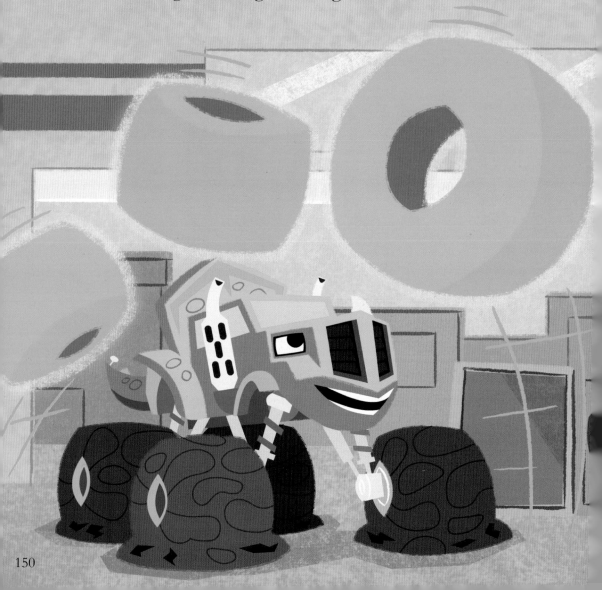

Zeg put on the tires—and started bouncing!
"Blaze? AJ? We have a problem," said
Gabby. "Those tires are the silliest tires of all!
They're super-bouncy tires. Once they start
bouncing, they don't stop!"

"Okay, tires," said Zeg. "No more bouncing!"

But the tires didn't stop. Zeg bounced out of the garage—and straight into traffic!

"Don't worry, Gabby," said Blaze. "We'll find a way to stop those bouncy tires."

"If we're gonna catch Zeg," said AJ, "we need to use Blazing Speed!"

Blaze revved his engine, popped his boosters, and—*VROOM!*—took off to save his friend!

"I know how we can save Zeg," said Blaze.
"Let's make those bouncy tires stick to the road.
We'll use adhesion! Adhesion is when two things
stick together."

Blaze unrolled a piece of tape and stuck it right
in Zeg's path.

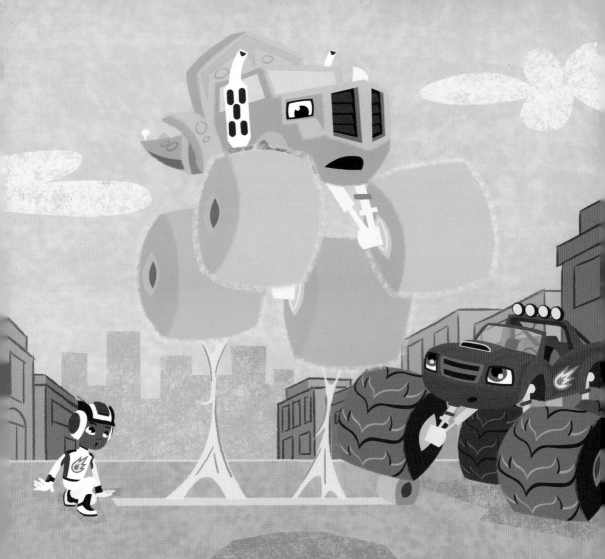

Zeg landed on the tape, but he bounced off again!
The tape was sticky, but not sticky enough.

"Next time we try adhesion, we need something
even stickier," AJ said.

Zeg kept bouncing straight toward a building.

"Uh-oh!" said Blaze. "That's the egg warehouse!"

Zeg crashed through the warehouse, knocking over crates and baskets. "Sorry! Coming through!" he yelled.

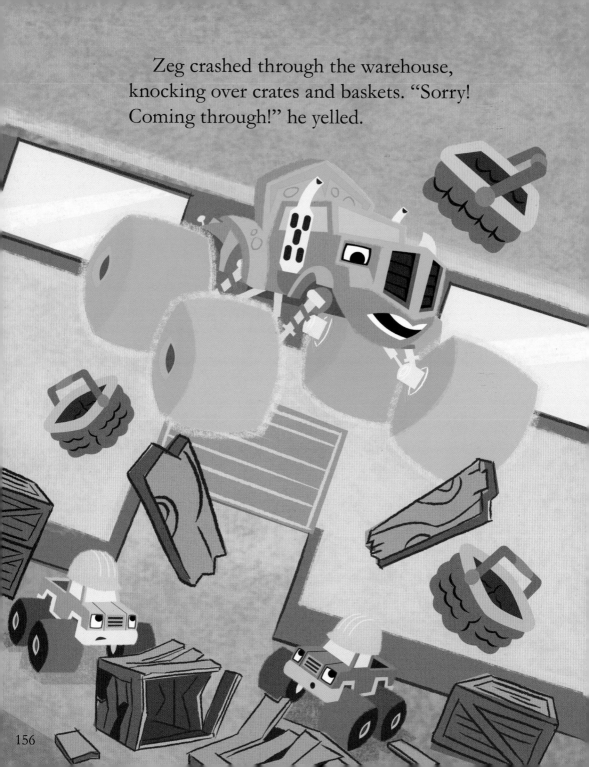

The bouncy tires hit a red button. A crane
turned and picked up a huge egg.

"Oh, no!" cried a worker truck. "He just
turned on the Giant Egg Dropper!"

The crane was going to drop the egg, so Blaze
raced as fast as he could to save it. He ducked
under conveyor belts and weaved past fallen
crates and baskets.

When the egg dropped, Blaze reached out
and caught it just in time!

Blaze had saved the giant egg, but he still had
to save Zeg.

"We can use adhesion again to stop those tires. Maybe this is sticky enough to work." AJ grabbed a bottle and squeezed out a puddle of glue.

Zeg landed in the glue. The goo splattered all over the tires and slowed Zeg down. But then he sprang up . . . and up . . . and up . . . until—*SNAP!*—he broke free! Just like the tape, the glue couldn't stop his bouncing!

"We're gonna need something even stickier," said AJ.

"Oh, no!" groaned Zeg. The super-bouncy
tires were taking him straight toward a bakery—
and a beautiful frosted cake!

"Somebody stop him!" cried the baker.

"I've got an idea," said Blaze. "What if we use quick-dry cement? That's the super-stickiest thing I can think of!"

Blaze put together a spiral mixing blade, a rotating drum, and a discharge chute, transforming himself into a cement mixer.

"The sticky cement is mixed and ready to pour!" called AJ.

Blaze tipped the discharge chute. Cement flowed out in a goopy gray puddle.

Zeg plunged into the puddle. Cement
flew up—but Zeg stayed down. The cement
was so sticky that Zeg couldn't bounce out!
"Adhesion worked!" AJ cheered.
"Zeg thank Blaze and AJ!" the dinosaur
truck said with a smile.

"You're welcome, big fella!" said Blaze. "Now, what do you say we get you a different set of tires?"

The dinosaur truck nodded. "Zeg like that idea! Zeg like!"

Back at the garage, Gabby replaced the bouncy tires with regular tires. "How do they feel?" she asked.

"Wheeee!" Zeg shouted as he cruised around the garage. "No bouncing!"

Blaze and AJ laughed, glad their friend was safely back on the ground!

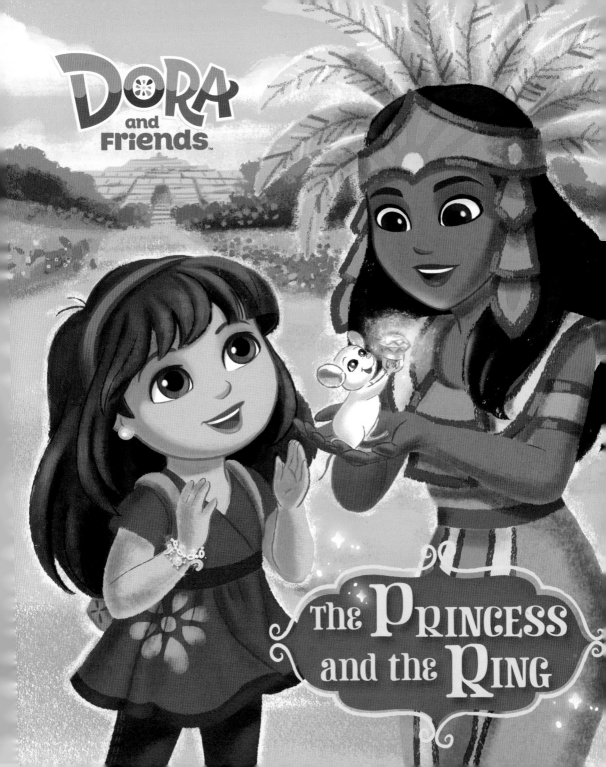

One day, Dora and Naiya were leaving a kindergarten class after reading the children a story about ancient treasure. Suddenly, Pablo rushed up to them. He had found a beautiful gold ring!

Naiya admired it. "That looks like the ancient treasure from our story!"

"Cool!" said Pablo. He slipped the ring on his finger.

There was a puff of smoke.

Dora and Naiya looked around. Pablo had
disappeared!

"Down here!" called Pablo. He had shrunk!

"There must have been a spell on the ring!"
said Naiya.

Pablo was worried. "I can't stay this size. I'm supposed to have story time with the kids!"

Dora crouched down. "*No te preocupes, Pablo. We'll figure out how to break the spell so you can be big again.*"

Naiya studied the ring. "Let's go to the library. I bet we can find out where this ring came from."

In the library, the three friends found a book that showed a picture of Pablo's ring. They learned that the ring had been a special present to a princess from her mother. A spell protected the magic ring. If anyone other than the princess wore it, he or she would shrink!

One day, a greedy wizard who worked for the princess stole the ring. A little mouse named Mousey saw the wizard put it on and shrink! The wizard was so tiny, he dropped the ring and lost it.

"'The spell cannot be broken until whoever has the ring puts it on the finger of the princess,'" read Dora.

"Pablo, can you show us where you found the ring?" asked Naiya.

Pablo led them to a city garden. Next to it was a very old wall. When Dora held the ring up to the wall, a tiny door appeared. It was a doorway to the princess's world!

But when Pablo tried to take the ring through the door, it was too big for him to carry by himself!

"We've all got to shrink so we can help you return the ring!" said Dora. She put the ring on, and she shrank, too.

Naiya put the ring on next. *Poof!* Now all three friends were ready for their big adventure. They picked up the ring and went through the doorway.

Dora, Naiya, and Pablo found themselves on
the busy streets of an ancient city.

"Wow, everything looks so big!" Pablo said.
He started to walk down the middle of the street.

Dora pulled him back. "We can't be seen
so small—someone will think we've stolen the
ring from the princess." She spotted a mouse
hole. "We can hide in there. C'mon!"

Inside the mouse hole, the three friends met
Mousey from the story of the princess and the
ring! Mousey offered them a ride to the palace to
return the ring to the princess.

"We have to watch out for the wizard and
his cat—they're looking for the ring," Mousey
warned as they set off.

As Dora and her friends traveled through
the city streets, the wizard spotted them. He
started to chase them!

Mousey turned a corner and lost the wizard.
But he was going so fast, the ring went flying.

It landed on the edge of a seesaw. Two men
moved the seesaw, and the ring flew into the
air again!

"Catch it, catch it, catch it!" called Dora.
She and her friends held their hands up . . . and
caught the ring!

With the ring safe, Mousey raced to the
royal palace.

When they arrived, Mousey led them to the
princess's bedroom. The princess was taking
a nap.

"How are we gonna get up there?" asked
Pablo, staring at the huge bed.

Naiya spotted a teacup and a spoon on a table
next to the bed. "We can make a seesaw!"

The friends climbed onto the table and balanced the spoon on the teacup. Then Mousey scurried up and jumped onto the spoon, catapulting them right onto the princess's pillow!

184

Dora, Naiya, and Pablo went over to slip
the ring onto the princess's finger. Suddenly,
the wizard's cat jumped onto the bed. The tiny
wizard leapt off his cat and put his hand on
the ring, too!

The princess woke up just as everyone
turned big again.

"Princess! These are the thieves who stole
your ring!" declared the wizard.

"No, Your Highness! The wizard took the
ring!" said Dora.

The princess shook her head. "He's my royal
wizard—he wouldn't do that." She called the
palace guards.

As the guards were taking Dora and her friends away, Mousey jumped in front of the princess. The princess threw up her hands in surprise—and the ring flew off!

Mousey picked up the ring and
ran out of the room. The princess,
the guards, the wizard and his cat, and
Dora and her friends followed close behind.

189

Mousey led everyone to the wizard's hut and squeezed under the door. The princess opened the door and gasped. Inside were piles of treasure that the wizard had been stealing from her!

"Guards, take the wizard and his cat away!"
declared the princess. She turned to Dora and
her friends. "Thank you for returning my ring.
It is very special to me."

The princess gave Dora, Pablo, and Naiya
gold medals as rewards. And she decided to keep
Mousey as her royal pet!

"Thanks for breaking the spell," Pablo told
his friends. "Now I'm big enough for story time
for the kids!"

"I think we have a great story for them,"
Dora said with a smile. "The story of how we
returned the ring and broke the spell together!
¡Todos juntos!"

BUBBLE GUPPIES

THE DOCTOR IS IN!

On her way to school one morning, Oona saw her friend Avi. He was riding his tricycle. *"Vroom! Vroom!"* Avi said. "Look how fast I can go!"

Suddenly, Avi hit a rock and fell off his tricycle!
"Ow!" Avi cried. "Mommy, my tail fin hurts."
"You'll be okay, honey," said Avi's mommy.
"But we'd better call the doctor, just to make sure."

Oona waved
goodbye as Avi
took a ride to
the hospital
with his
mommy . . . in a
clambulance.

When Oona got to class, she told everyone about Avi's accident.

"The doctor will take good care of him," said Mr. Grouper. "He'll probably take an X-ray."

"What's an X-ray?" Gil asked.
"An X-ray is a picture of your bones,"
said Nonny.

"Do we have bones?" Oona asked.

"You sure do, Guppies," Mr. Grouper said. "Bones are the hard things you feel under your skin. They help support and protect you."

"Without your bones, you couldn't stand up,

jump,

or swim."

"I went to the doctor once," said Deema. "She made me stick out my tongue and say 'Ahhh!'"

"The doctor was checking your throat to make sure it was okay," said Mr. Grouper.

"What else do doctors do?" asked Oona.
"Let's think about it," said Mr. Grouper.

"Sometimes a doctor uses a special flashlight to look in your ear," said Oona.

"And sometimes a doctor will use a stethoscope to listen to your heart," said Gil.

"He or she will probably take your temperature with a thermometer," said Nonny.

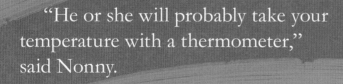

"You might have to get a shot," said Deema.

"Shots hurt," said Nonny.

"Only a little bit," said Mr. Grouper. "But they keep you from getting sick."

"Oona, would you like to visit Avi in the hospital?"
Mr. Grouper asked.

"We can bring him a balloon," Molly said.

Oona thought that was a great idea.

The Bubble Guppies lined up, and Mr. Grouper led them to the hospital. They saw doctors and nurses there, and patients who were getting better.

The Bubble Guppies and Mr. Grouper found Avi's room. Avi was in a big, comfy bed. His mother and his doctor were with him.

Avi was happy to see his friends.
Everyone wanted to know how he
was feeling.

"Avi will be fine," the doctor said. "He broke a bone in his tail fin, but we fixed him right up."

The doctor showed everyone Avi's X-ray.

And Avi showed everyone his cast! The doctor had
put it on Avi's tail fin to help his bone heal.

"Who wants to sign my cast?" Avi asked.

The Bubble Guppies took turns signing their names and drawing pictures on Avi's cast.

When they were done, the doctor
said Avi could go home!